Does this book you  ?

Yup!

Then you can write your name here:

....

Ready
to
Read?

Yup!

Make Music

by
Ted Dewan

HarperCollins *Children's Books*

Round the corner,
Not far away,
Bing's been bongo-ing all day.

Let's make music.
What will we play?

rice tub

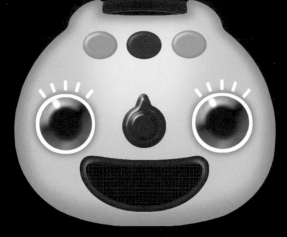

music box

keys

bell

tube

Pick one!

All
ready?

YUP!

YUP!

beep!

OK.
Let's play!

Rice goes shaka shaka

beep!

Keys go
jingle
jing

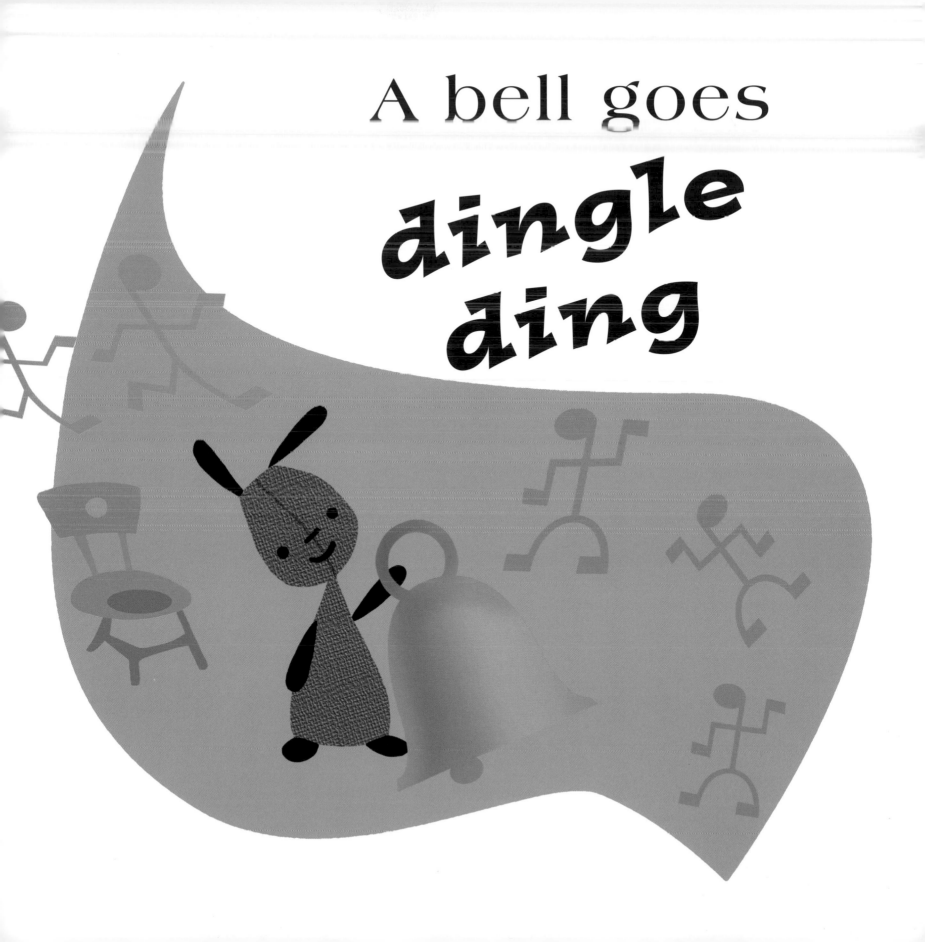

A bell goes

dingle
ding

Bing goes

BINGO! BONGO! BANG!

Don't go bongo, Bing.

Bing goes

**BINGO!
BONGO!
BANG!**

Don't go
bongo,
Bing!

BANGO!

BONGO!

No, Bing! No! Don't go...

Oh NO.
Poor music box is
broken.

Maybe we can mend it, Bing.

And then, together...

Making music.
It's a Bing Thing.

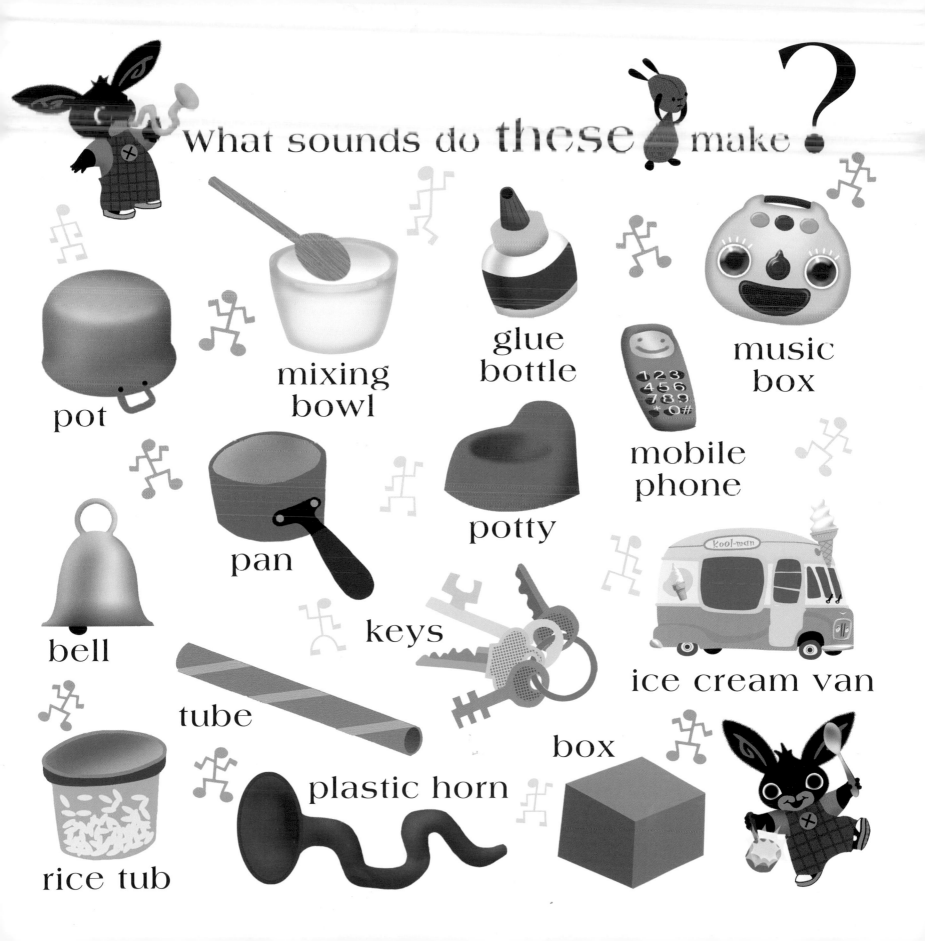

What sounds do these make?

pot

mixing bowl

glue bottle

music box

mobile phone

bell

pan

potty

ice cream van

tube

keys

rice tub

plastic horn

box

Bing again?
Yup!

978-0-00-751477-9

Get Dressed

978-0-00-751479-3

Bed Time

978-0-00-751540-0

Something for Daddy

by
Ted Dewan

First published in hardback in Great Britain by David Fickling Books in 2004. This edition published in paperback by HarperCollins Children's Books in 2014.   5 7 9 10 8 6 4   ISBN: 978-0-00-751542-4
HarperCollins Children's Books is a division of HarperCollins Publishers Ltd. Text and illustrations copyright © Ted Dewan 2004, 2014. The author/illustrator asserts the moral right to be identified as the author/illustrator of the work.
A CIP catalogue record for this title is available from the British Library. All rights reserved. No part of this publication may be reproduced, stored in a retrieval system, or transmitted in any form or by any means electronic, mechanical, photocopying, recording or otherwise, without the prior permission of HarperCollins Publishers Ltd, 77-85 Fulham Palace Road, Hammersmith, London W6 8JB. Visit our website at: www.harpercollins.co.uk. Printed and bound in Spain